For Nora Bartlett because she loves horses
—J.Y.

For my daughter Morgan
—R.S.

Text copyright © 2010 by Jane Yolen
Illustrations copyright © 2010 by Ruth Sanderson

All rights reserved. Published in the United States by Random House Children's Books, a division of Random House, Inc., New York.

Random House and the colophon are registered trademarks of Random House, Inc.

Visit us on the Web! www.randomhouse.com/kids

Educators and librarians, for a variety of teaching tools, visit us at www.randomhouse.com/teachers

Library of Congress Cataloging-in-Publication Data
Yolen, Jane.
Hush, little horsie / by Jane Yolen ; illustrated by Ruth Sanderson. — 1st ed.
p. cm.
Summary: Rhyming text assures foals that their mothers are watching over them while they
leap on a farm, frolic on a beach, gallop on a plain, and sleep in a stall.
ISBN 978-0-375-85853-6 (trade) — ISBN 978-0-375-95853-3 (lib. bdg.)
[1. Stories in rhyme. 2. Bedtime—Fiction. 3. Horses—Fiction.] I. Sanderson, Ruth, ill. II. Title.
PZ8.3.Y76 Hus 2010
[E]—dc22
2008030184

MANUFACTURED IN MALAYSIA

10 9 8 7 6 5 4 3 2 1

First Edition

Hush, Little Horsie

written by Jane Yolen

illustrated by Ruth Sanderson

RANDOM HOUSE 🏠 NEW YORK

Hush, little horsie,
Asleep on the farm.
Your mama is near
And will keep you from harm.

She'll watch when you run,
And she'll watch when you leap.

And when you are tired,
She'll watch as you sleep.

Hush, little horsie,
Asleep on the plain.
Your mama will shade you
From sunshine and rain.

She'll watch when you gallop,
She'll watch when you leap.

And when you are tired,
She'll watch as you sleep.

Hush, little horsie,
Asleep by the sea.
Your mama stands guard
So your dreams can run free.

She'll watch when you frolic,
She'll watch when you leap.

And when you are tired,
She'll watch as you sleep.

Hush, little horsie,
Asleep on the moor.
Your mama is close—
That's what mamas are for.

She'll watch when you play,
And she'll watch when you leap.

And when you are tired,
She'll watch as you sleep.

Hush, little horsie,
Asleep in the stall.
Your mama is waiting
In case you should call.

She'll watch when you prance,
And she'll watch when you leap.

And when you are tired,
She'll watch as you sleep.

Hush, little darling,
Right here on the bed—
You cuddle your horsie
While stories are read.

When lights are turned out,
Into dreams you both leap.
Then I can watch faithfully
While you're asleep.